CUSTOMER SERVICE
AND OTHER STORIES

T0349388

CUSTOMER SERVICE
AND OTHER STORIES

LINDA MARTIN

CANADA

Publisher's note: This book is a work of fiction. Names, characters, places and incidents are either the product of the author's imagination or are used fictitiously, and any resemblance to actual persons living or dead is entirely coincidental.

In *Barrio*, a few reminiscences came from the book, *Walking Through Barrio Anita's History "una familia unida."* Tucson, Arizona. Barrio Anita Neighborhood Assn., 2001, and were slightly altered for literary purposes.

Library and Archives Canada Cataloguing in Publication

Title: Customer service and other stories / Linda Martin.

Names: Martin, Linda, 1950– author.

Description: Includes index.

Identifiers: Canadiana (print) 20240382641 | Canadiana (ebook) 2024038265x |
ISBN 9781989689769 (softcover) | ISBN 9781989689806 (EPUB)

Subjects: LCGFT: Short stories.

Classification: LCC PS8626.A77244 C87 2024 | DDC C813/.6—dc23

Printed and bound in Canada on 100% recycled paper.

Now Or Never Publishing
901, 163 Street, Surrey, British Columbia, Canada V4A 9T8

nonpublishing.com
Fighting Words.

We gratefully acknowledge the support of the Canada Council for the Arts
and the British Columbia Arts Council for our publishing program.

Table of Contents

Barrio I

Customer Service II

Development 19

Faking It 27

Grand Canyon Tour 35

Great Salt Lake 43

Intermission 49

Pool 57

Poverty Day 63

Sequoia 71

Thanksgiving 81

Welland Canal 87

BARRIO

When she inherited her grandmother's house on Rudolpho Street in a Tucson barrio, Victoria warned her husband, Leo, that the old neighbourhood was full of ghosts. Her grandmother had lived there in the 1940s and 50s. It was where her mother was born and grew up.

Chica, how can you marry a white man? her friends had asked. But Victoria told them that Leo had soul. *He's an artist, and hot like Ernesto was,* she insisted, referring to her high school boyfriend.

Leo and Victoria met in college. Both were in the fine arts program and there was an immediate attraction.

Hey. I'm not worried about some superstitious nonsense, Leo said. *We're so lucky to get a home in such a central neighbourhood. You know they're going for a million now? Though there's still a lot of empty lots. It's a shame more of the other adobe houses weren't saved.*

Yeah, the location is great and I love the house. But you'll see, this place is haunted.

If it's your grandmother—who cares? You told me Yolanda was a nice old lady. Maybe she'll bring us luck.

It's not Yolanda who spooks me. It's the history of this place. They say there was an Apache burial ground here. I've heard the weird stories my mother used to tell. She said that one of her classmates, Rosa, took a short cut home through a cotton field. There used to be farms where the expressway is now. She saw a black woman standing by a shed. Her face was lined with bloody scratches and she was foaming at the mouth. Rosa ran away screaming but couldn't resist looking back. There was no shed and no woman, only some tall weeds.

Another story was about a cleaner who worked at the school in the 1940s. She was angry at a little Mexican girl, locked her in a closet and forgot about her. That girl died. At night, people have seen the illuminated outline of a person in the school window. Some have seen this girl flying over the school roof.

Come on, Victoria, you know these are exaggerations. You come from a rich culture full of magical stories. But who really believes them?

Maybe so, but Yolanda herself told the story about her dead mother coming into the kitchen and asking for a cup of coffee. When she handed it to her, my great-grandmother disappeared.

It's all imagination. You took the same psychology class I did. Remember the lecture on visual input, memories and perception?

Okay. I see your point. Let's start unpacking these boxes. I need dishes and cutlery. My parents are dropping by for dinner tonight. My dad's going to put in a new drain pipe under the sink and my mom is bringing some curtains she sewed for the bedroom window.

At promptly six o'clock Francis and Ralph knocked on the front door. *Victoria, mi pollita,* her mother embraced her.

Papa come in. Wait till you see what we've done to the place!

It's already obvious. Such beautiful red flowers and the tall cactus. I like how you decorated the wall with jars, vines and birds.

The family turned to look out at the front yard. The cactus had been there since before Yolanda's time. Victoria planted the Firecracker flowers. Leo had painted the front door magenta. It was becoming an area of artists and artisans. Each house on their street was renovated with a creative flair.

Inside was a mix of old and new. Yolanda's pine dining room table and hutch had been refinished and oiled. Some of her embroidered pillows were on the new Ikea sofa. A small collection of Cabat pottery was on a shelf in the kitchen. Her grandmother had an artistic side, something Victoria felt she inherited.

Mija, I love how you've designed the house, said her mother. *That yellow in the living room—like sunshine and such a deep blue in the kitchen—like the sky.*

Victoria cooked carne marinated in lime and garlic; served it with a corn and tomato salad that was her father's favourite. Leo had learned to bake pan dulces. He brought the warm fruit buns in a basket to the table for dessert.

Carina, how happy you and Leo will be in this home, Ralph looked around with satisfaction. *All I need is a strong coffee and I'll get to work on that drain.*

I'll make it, said Francis. They could hear the whirr of the grinder in the kitchen and soon the aroma of fresh café con leche drifted into the dining room. Leo helped carry the steaming cups to the table.

Mamma, I've been telling Leo about the fantasmas in the neighbourhood. He doesn't think they are real. Just stories.

Ah si, who knows if any are left now? If people don't believe, it's hard for the spirits. There are fewer places on the planet where they are welcome. The spirits float away like dreams. Everything is paved over now. Before, there was so much dust stirred up by the desert winds, no wonder the spirits rose.

Francis. Have you ever seen a ghost? Leo demanded.

Of course. I saw La Llorana with her long hair, in her white dress. Our family was playing cards, here at this very table. We could hear a woman crying "Ah mis hijos—where are my children?" Then we saw her for an instant.

Victoria, tell Leo about Estella's great grandson, what was his name?

Oh yes, Roberto. When Estella was a little girl she saw an old Indian woman grinding corn in the corner of her grandmother's bedroom. The grandmother said Estella was loco but decided to dig up the floor in that corner. She found a ceramic pot filled with coins. Years later, Roberto heard feet shuffling on the porch near where the pot was found.

Ridiculous. Enough of these tales, Leo wagged his finger at them. *If there is a ghost in this house, we can take a selfie with it and start a blog.*

You young people can laugh but I miss the old days.

Tell us how it was then, said Leo.

We knew all the neighbours. If someone was sick they would bring you soup, if someone died, the coffin stayed in the living room for a few days. Lots of the houses had dirt floors. They were sprinkled with water to keep down the dust. In the summer we slept outside under the ramada. There are fences everywhere now. We never used to lock the door.

We played baseball in the park, Ralph chimed in from the kitchen. *We made money returning bottles we collected from the rich on Snob Hill. I had a shoe shine stand for a while, then sold oranges for a dollar a day.*

Parties, lots of parties, Francis remembered. *We danced to Elvis at the Del Rio Ballroom. Our mothers warned, Manzana mordida no vendera—an apple that has been bitten will not sell. Women wore open safety pins on the hem of their skirts so if men tried to fondle them they got pricked.*

Victoria laughed and Leo said, *Ouch.* Ralph came back from the kitchen and sat down at the table.

Okay. It was an easy fix. No more leak. You've got me thinking about the past. Do you remember, Francis, when there were falcons, skunks and javelinas in the arroyos? We boys made flutes from reed stalks.

Yes. There used to be sunflowers blooming everywhere in the barrio. Do you recall the view to the mountains from the park and the swimming pool? Now we can only see cars and trucks zooming by. In those times the pool had days for blacks and browns only. The school was segregated too and we weren't allowed to speak Spanish.

At least the school is still there. I hear it's bilingual now. So when can we expect grandchildren?

Please, dad, we just got married! Victoria protested, but Leo squeezed her shoulder and smiled.

I miss the hardware store, said Ralph. *Everyone drives now so I guess it doesn't matter. You know when the grocery closed, the building was taken over by the Hernandez family. I was talking to Louie and he said they are selling over 300 dozen fresh tortillas a day to restaurants.*

Wow. I didn't know that. We've been in there to pick up lunch but I had no idea they were producing on that scale. Maybe more businesses will open up if the area is re-populated.

The lots aren't selling so fast, said Francis who spent a few years in real estate. *It's the location between the expressway and the railway tracks.*

I think the neighbourhood will take off, said Leo. *My generation likes to live downtown. And look at the houses that have already been renovated. They're really posh.*

Anyway, we should be going now, Ralph said. *I've got a big job tomorrow up north. Mamma wants me to retire but I'm not ready.*

Victoria walked her parents to the door while Leo cleared the table and loaded the dishwasher.

—

In the backyard of their house, Leo and Victoria had built a small studio out of corrugated metal. The front of the structure had two large doors that swung outward, so that in the good weather, it was like working in the open air. A mature Netleaf Hackberry shaded much of the yard making it comfortable to work in the heat.

Both Leo and Victoria were able to support themselves with their work. They made decorative wall art, like suns and crosses from copper, garden ornaments, and smaller tabletop items like paperweights and trivets. Occasionally, they were commissioned by wealthy clients to do intricate designs on gates or to create larger statement pieces like horses or birds. Mostly, the results were standard with market appeal. When they were each involved in creating something personal and unique, they often discussed line, movement, balance, kinetics and spatial relation-ships, to clarify their ideas. Leo preferred the look of raw metal. Victoria enjoyed experimenting with colour.

You know, I've been thinking about the idea of a ghost sculpture. In fact, wouldn't it be interesting if we both created our own version of what that would look like. If nothing else we can use them for grave markers.

Estúpido, estúpido, estúpido, Victoria shouted at him, causing the thrushes to fly out of the Hackberry. *You've just cursed us!*

What are you talking about? Leo was genuinely surprised at the force of her reaction. *It's the twenty-first century. What are you afraid of?*

You're inviting the dead into our studio, our yard, our home!

It's a fricking hunk of metal. Get over it. Then more softly he said, *It's okay. I'll do this project myself. You don't have to be involved.*

Leo stood at his worktable and began making drawings. He was intrigued by the story of the weeping woman and decided to sculpt her. He would use copper for the most part, but the tears, he thought, should be made out of pre-rusted steel. He would polish them with linseed and turpentine to give them a beautiful sheen.

Victoria had retreated to the kitchen. She made herself a cup of calming tea and sat at the table drinking it. It took a while for her to stop shaking. *Why am I so upset?* she asked herself. *Maybe I really am overreacting.* Victoria returned to the studio. She would make a few small scale flower pendants to hang on a necklace and brush on some of the leftover paint to make them vibrant.

They worked in silence, concentrating and lost in their own thoughts. Contrite, Leo offered to make dinner that night and served up a beef stir fry loaded with onions and peppers. Victoria still seemed distracted and he had trouble engaging her in conversation. After dinner, she became absorbed in a book and Leo went back to the studio to complete his drawings. She was still remote when he came to bed and turned away from him when he tried to embrace her. He believed she'd be over this mood by the morning, but in fact it took several weeks for her to warm up to him again.

By the next spring, Victoria was pregnant. Her parents were elated and brought baskets of pomegranates, peaches and mangoes. Leo was excited and solicitous. In between working on the weeping woman, which was almost done, he built a small cradle and made two rattles out of empty gourds. Victoria painted them with bright patterns.

In July, Leo found a buyer for the large sculpture. It was in fact, going to be used in a cemetery as the centerpiece of a newly created remembrance garden. Leo was paid handsomely for his work and talked with Victoria about taking a hiking trip to Sedona. They could buy some quality outdoor gear and stay at an upscale hotel with a heated pool. Victoria was beginning to show so they would do some easy walks and she could stay by the pool if she felt tired.

During the first couple of days, they were mesmerized by the tarnished red of the sandstone but on the third day Victoria said she wasn't feeling well and that evening she miscarried into the toilet of their hotel room. Leo couldn't help comparing the blood that poured out of her to the colour of the rocks. Things must have been going wrong with the baby's development for a while. Nothing came out that looked remotely like a fetus, only sad fragments of tissue.

You'll soon be pregnant again! soothed Victoria's mother. *You're young!*

Before you know it we'll be grandparents! her father reassured.

In bed, Leo made an extra effort to please her, aroused her again and again. She seemed even more passionate than before, as if she was accessing the very depths of her body. But months and then a year passed and there was nothing.

Business had been picking up since the Sedona trip. More retirees were moving to Tucson and renovating some of the more modest homes and condos around the city. Leo couldn't keep up with orders for garden sculptures, not to mention some of the decorative ironwork he was providing for civic buildings. So he hired an assistant.

Victoria no longer shared the studio which was overcrowded with Leo's tools and scrap metal. She rented her own space not far from downtown. Her reputation as an artist was growing and she doubled her output. A few prominent galleries in Phoenix had discovered her talent and were selling her jewelry and ornaments.

Victoria's parents rarely saw their daughter now, even though they admonished, *Don't be a stranger.*

And Leo said half-jokingly, *We'll have to start making appointments to see each other.*

When Victoria was home, Leo caught glimpses of her crying now and then. Sometimes it was when she was scattering bird seed in the yard; sometimes when the light caught her eye; sometimes when she tipped the watering can towards a flower. When he asked about her sculpture, she was vague, said she was working on a special project but that he would know when it was finished.

CUSTOMER SERVICE

Sandra enjoyed looking at online real estate. She scrolled through some of the high-end listings, like the eight million dollar penthouse in Yorkville with custom maple cabinetry in the kitchen, and a gas fireplace in every room. The twelve-million dollar beauty in Rosedale had a glass exterior at the back that stepped down into a wooded ravine. There was an indoor lap pool visible from the terrace. The agent described the home as a *masterpiece*. The fourteen-million dollar gem in Forest Hill was billed as the *ultimate in luxury* and contained a home theatre, indoor tennis and basketball court, wine cellar and ten bathrooms. But most incredible was the thirty-five million dollar palace in the Bridle Path. It had hand forged wrought iron railings; a courtyard with fountain; grand salon and ballroom; mahogany ceiling and walls in the office; a stained glass skylight in the upper hall; and a porcelain bathtub with gold filigree in the master.

After she had her fill of these amazing mansions, Sandra looked at more affordable options. Then she checked out the photos of the agents that accompanied the ads, and chose a pleasant-looking guy, probably in his forties, to work with. She phoned and left a message and he returned the call a few hours later, introducing himself as Trevor. Sandra explained that she was looking for a one-bedroom apartment because she had to downsize. She specified mid-town and mid-price. Trevor said he would line up a few places.

They met two days later at the first apartment. Trevor was tall and lean but didn't carry his height well. He was dressed in a suit even though it was a sweltering day. The apartment had blue-shag carpeting, a snot-green counter in the kitchen and pink appliances in the bathroom.

It can be updated, Trevor said.

Sandra suppressed a snigger. Trevor locked up and they headed to his car for the drive to the next place. He opened the car door for Sandra and she found herself inside a vintage Cadillac. Now this was customer service! After an exhausting afternoon, viewing a cupboard billed as a den, popcorn ceilings, and a building with a marble lobby complete with a Scarlett O'Hara staircase, they called it a day.

Sandra agreed to be profiled and receive emails from Trevor. He also checked in regularly by phone to see if Sandra wanted to see any of the listings. Every couple of weeks she agreed to meet with him to see another round of the dreary, box-like condos. Sandra was careful not to take up his time on weekends or evenings.

She enjoyed their conversation as he drove efficiently through traffic in the air-conditioned car.

I worked as a concierge and a taxi driver and some other jobs before I got married. But my wife wanted me to be more ambitious. She's an X-ray technician and is applying for medical school.

Sandra heard the pride in his voice.

Well, you make sure you give her lots of support and be there for her when she needs you.

When Trevor tried to get Sandra to talk about herself, she dismissed him with, *Oh, I'm not very interesting. Just your typical old lady. Since my husband died, I don't need such a large home.* This was a lie, because Sandra was divorced and already living in a condo.

On Sundays, Sandra went to the open houses to satisfy her interest in architectural details, furniture design and use of space. Each week she chose another neighbourhood. She preferred the higher end sales because many of them were new builds and had the latest in flooring, windows, appliances and bathroom fixtures. The builders were using a lot of beech and hemlock flooring these days. Pendant lights were still popular although chandeliers seemed to be making a comeback. Also, the more exclusive homes had fewer people wandering through so Sandra could stand back and survey a room without being jostled.

One Sunday, a couple of months after signing on with Trevor, Sandra stepped into the living room of a modern town home with floor to ceiling windows, polished concrete floors, an

Ethan Allen Preston sofa and several tribal rugs placed just so by the stager. She noticed Trevor too late. She could tell by his frown that he was confused about why she was there. Sandra wasn't in the mood to make excuses. She hurried out the front door before he had a chance to speak with her.

Sandra was ready for a change of pace anyway. She might go shopping at Holts. She owned a smart Burberry that she had splurged on years ago when she was single, and in London. The crystal earrings that her first husband bought her had kept their dazzle and looked more expensive than they really were. She'd recently had a cut and blow dry so her hair looked styled. She could stop in the cosmetics department on her way to the exclusive designer collections, for a spritz of perfume and a free makeup session.

She had studied the advertising brochure, promoting resort wear, which recently came in the mail. The models were reed thin but Sandra had kept her figure so that wouldn't be a problem. She could say she was going to be cruising the Mediterranean. Sandra would try on the crochet lace, large leaf patterned, sleeveless tea gown in black and white, priced at nine thousand dollars; or the Prada, sable Leggero rabbit print with feathers at the wrist. The top cost a thousand, and the pants, gold trimmed around the ankles were three thousand. Or she could get the same outfit in a peony print and silver trim at the ankles. It might be fun to sample the nylon tech socks for two-hundred bucks, paired with the Decollete Spaazzolato white heeled sandals for fifteen hundred. The sales people would be very attentive and overly flattering, saying how envious they were about her upcoming trip and asking what ports of call were on the tour.

But ultimately, Sandra decided she was more in the mood to check out cars. A year ago it was BMWs. She looked up Porsches this time. On the web there was a list of dealerships. Sandra would have to dress up for this too, show she could afford a car in the luxury category. She had a good string of pearls from her grandmother and an impressive sized ring that looked like a real diamond. Sandra's navy serge suit that she wore to job interviews and now wore to funerals was classic. She chose the flat heeled imitation Louboutins so she could test drive. It was always a rush for her to get behind the wheel of a beautifully engineered vehicle.

The automatic doors slid open as she entered the dealership. A very young salesman was free to help her out. He introduced himself as Jack. She gave her name in return. Jack was so obliging, offering her a premium coffee before he began squiring her around to each of the models in the showroom.

Show me everything, she told him. *Yes, it's for myself.*

They looked at a butter yellow Carrera with a Cabriolet body. The price was obscene. A bright red Boxter had the Super Sound package complete with 12 loudspeakers. The salesman, who had a neat beard, possibly to appear older, opened the door, had her sit in the leather seats, and showed off the automatic everything. Sandra admired the silver Targa which had excellent ergonomics and a choice of carbon, aluminum or high quality wood interior trim. In the end she said she wanted to test drive the turquoise Cayman. It was in a lower price range and she was timid about handling anything above $100,000.

Jack led Sandra to the demo car and she got in behind the wheel. The dealership was in an industrial area so traffic was light and there were no pedestrians.

God, this handles well, Sandra remarked to Jack.

Great car, he responded. *If you pull over here, and let me take over for a few blocks, I'll show you some features you're really going to like.*

Jack started driving towards the highway that connected up with the last street in the area.

I remember you loved that 428 Gran Turismo BMW. What do you think of this by comparison?

What do you mean? How did you know? Sandra was startled.

I used to work that dealership.

Jack was taking an off ramp that exited to a rural area.

I think I have a good sense of this car now. I don't think we need to go any further.

What's the rush? I spent two hours with you when you were considering that BMW. You didn't buy anything or get back to me. I lost another sale because of that.

I'm sorry. I'm trying to recall this.

I've grown a beard since then. And by the way, my name isn't Jack. It's Carl. You know, there really is some truth in the fact that lots of people choose occupations that correspond to their names.

Then Sandra remembered. She had said these very words to Carl about names. He floored the pedal.

Shouldn't we be heading back? Sandra's anxiety was increasing.

Not yet. First, I'm going to take you for a ride, madam. I've got some time to kill.

DEVELOPMENT

The sign was up. A fifty-storey building, adjacent to Frank's home, was proposed. It felt like an invasion. It was perceived by many of his neighbours as a threat. They attended the public meetings organized by the well-meaning city councillor. At first, these held out hope. There was a chance to hear the municipal planner, a smartly dressed, articulate woman with tidy hair and spike heels. She mouthed a stream of platitudes about guidelines on height and density that were legally unenforceable and thus meaningless. Residents were encouraged to step up to the microphone to deliver passionate outbursts or measured speeches protesting the high-rise, but this was mere appeasement.

The neighbouring houses of which Frank's was one, would lose their view of the sky. A treed slope, representing a small but significant green space would be demolished. Hawks, groundhogs, squirrels, foxes, skunks and bees would lose their habitat.

Frank liked to sit for hours, on his back porch. Cardinals, blue jays and robins flew from yew to spruce, pleasing to the eye and the soul. He couldn't imagine how this pleasure would continue with a backdrop of concrete. Frank often watched the sunset from his living room window. The high-rise would block this view.

Frank had owned a barber shop, but retired when his rent increased and he was eligible for a pension. He hadn't stayed in touch with any of his employees, and hadn't married or had children. Frank liked living alone. His neighbours didn't pry, but if they passed by, while he was gardening, they talked planting, pruning, seeds and weeds. In his backyard, he had thirteen varieties of roses. The colours ranged from deep vermillion to light pink. He grew basil, chives and mint in pots, and in the spring the plot by the fence was ablaze with forsythia.

The city claimed there were rules about shadowing but Frank worried about his flowers. Would they adjust to a different quality of light? Frank wondered if there would be compromises on setbacks, or root damage from excavations that would affect the health of his trees.

Frank was trimming the spirea and hydrangeas in his front yard, when his neighbour walked by.

Hey Frank, Dan called out to him. *Getting your garden ready for winter? The almanac says it's going to be a cold one. Not like last year when I was out in a sweater a couple of days in January.*

It's the global warming. You can't count on anything being the way it was, Frank replied.

Frank hadn't bothered with the internet thing or email. He preferred the radio, newspaper and TV for his information. But now that they were bringing in the development, he needed to have access to meeting information and updates. The local residents' association was doing its best to liaise with the city and developers. People chipped in for the cost of a lawyer to assist with the negotiations.

Frank hired a volunteer high school student, Jason, to help him buy a computer and show him how to use it.

You want to get an Apple, Jason said, as he led Frank into a brightly lit store with rows of counters lined with laptops. A salesperson gave Jason a number to type into his phone so they could get on the waiting list for service.

Would you be interested in a phone as well? Jason asked Frank. *You know it has a camera in it?*

No, no. I have a phone in my kitchen. It's all I need, Frank insisted.

After Frank got the laptop home, Jason came over and trained him to search.

Just pick a topic, Jason said. *You'll be amazed at the number of hits you'll get.*

And Frank was amazed. They searched for red rose trees and a row of photographs came up at the top of the screen followed by text highlighted in blue.

Now look here, said Jason, pointing to a number at the top of the page. *Your search resulted in 247,000 hits. But don't worry, the first couple of articles on the screen are the most relevant.*

Using a photocopied list, that Dan had given Frank, Jason showed him how to enter the email addresses of his neighbours and send a message to Dan. A few hours after Jason left, Frank heard the ding of an incoming message.

Welcome to the web. Never thought I'd see the day when you'd be using email—but hey, that's great. Sorry the message isn't more positive, but just got word that the meeting with the tribunal didn't go well. They've approved the fifty storeys. There's nothing more we can do to fight this. The builders will be breaking ground later this year.

It felt to Frank, like someone had punched him in the gut, and then the rage began to take over as he responded to Dan's email. He wrote *Dear Dan*, not realizing that this form of address was basically obsolete in the cyber world. *Thank you for informing me about this. I know people have to have a place to live, and this is near transit, but the rent will be so expensive, it will be unaffordable to those who need it most. The majority of the apartments will be too small to be suitable for families. The Premier of our province got rid of rent controls on all newly constructed buildings. How is this high-rise helping homelessness and the many thousands of people on waiting lists for public housing?*

Frank was still angry when he clicked on Google. Some cartoon characters danced around above the search box, but what he was looking for was serious. He got some results almost immediately, about the pros and cons of high-rise buildings. There were a couple of summaries of papers, presented by professors at conferences. Social and health risks were reviewed, as were the negative impacts on the biosphere. Concerns showed up in media reports about lack of infrastructure, traffic, green space, and integration with existing neighbourhoods.

In London, a residents' protest against high-rises led to a statement of concern that *never before have we built at such mass.* The British Prime Minister called the group *bourgeois nimbys.* In Vancouver, people who spoke out against losing their view of the mountains were considered heartless and insensitive to those less fortunate, even though condos in the proposed structure would be marketed to the rich.

Frank extended the search to see how others had dealt with these incursions. Apparently, in 2015, in Oregon, there was a neighbourhood group who were trying to save some Douglas

Firs and Sequoias slated for cutting in a new subdivision. They were able to make a deal with the developers and protect the Sequoias.

The trees that would come down in Frank's area were Norway Maples. They had a bad reputation as invasive species because their shade prevented seedlings from growing. But the shade was cooling, the trees provided habitat and the Norways could withstand urban pollution.

Frank typed in the words: trees, protests, protection and more articles appeared. He read about Earth First, a group that carried out spiking in the 1980s. They inserted small pieces of metal in tree trunks which damaged the chain saws and mill blades of loggers. They had a "puke-in" protest in a shopping mall and locked their bodies to trees and bulldozers.

He discovered the term "monkeywrenching" which involved sabotaging equipment that was environmentally damaging. Ecoterrorism started to turn up in his search results.

Frank read about the activists Red Cloud Thunder and about the Earth Liberation Front who protested the loss of a wooded wetland to a suburb in Seattle. They burned down the unoccupied new houses using milk jugs filled with gasoline, and fuses made from packs of matches. Frank took note of this.

He looked at the time in the corner of his screen which counted out the minutes. He had been sitting at his desk for two hours. He needed to get a drink of water, stretch his legs, check to see if any of the seedlings in his basement were germinating.

And then Frank asked himself this. Could he, in his old age, become subversive? Was he able to resort to extreme action even if it was just to create unease? What would it matter if he was arrested? Would he miss napping on his sofa or making a cup of tea when the mood arose? He would definitely miss gardening, but maybe he'd end up at one of those prisons that has a farm or landscaping opportunities.

Frank began saving milk jugs, storing gallon cans of gasoline in his garage, and buying matches. It was a large site and once construction began, there would be an extensive area to target.

Frank was almost eighty. He couldn't risk waiting for the project to progress. He would have to strike soon.

The demolition started on schedule. Within three months the small plaza on the corner was gone. Frank complained in an email to Dan that he would miss the convenience store, bank, pharmacy, hardware, several restaurants, the optometrist and chiropodist. He didn't mention how much his conversations with the shopkeepers had meant to him.

Dan replied, *Don't worry. Many services and shopping are done online anyways and you'll get used to it. Most items can be delivered right to your door. Have Jason come over again to help you get started.*

But Frank didn't contact Jason.

A huge pit formed at the bottom of Frank's garden. Then the trucks and excavators arrived. There was constant noise and dust in the air. Now would be the time to act. Concrete and steel don't burn in a gasoline fire, but vehicles could be destroyed.

Frank started planning. He didn't have to figure out how to access the site. The workers had cut a hole in the fence so they could slip through and lean against one of his maples, to have a smoke. Frank worked in the dark of late evening and started moving the gasoline cans from the garage. He stacked them under a tarp at the property line. Frank piled up the milk jugs beside them under another tarp. He had a small wagon for transporting the cartons to the base of the excavators and under the trucks. He carried the matches with him in a canvas bag. He was ready.

Frank waited for a moonless sky. His eyesight was weak so he needed to wear a head-lamp. It was the middle of the night and he was counting on his neighbours being deeply asleep. Frank began filling the jugs with gas. He could still back out, he told himself as he filled the final container.

I don't actually have to do this, he muttered, as he pulled the wagon to the first truck. Frank set his bag on the ground. When he was a boy, he would flip open a pack of matches, lick the tips, and taste the faint tang of sulphur. Frank reached down and took the matches from his bag, but didn't indulge that innocent pleasure.

FAKING IT

G avin, where is the whatchamacallit?
  What do you mean?
You know the thingamajig that turns on the TV.
You mean the zapper?
Yeah, that's it.
Gavin located it and brought it over to Lorraine.
When it was time to prepare dinner, she started floundering when she peeled the potatoes.
Darn, I can't get this skin off.
What do you mean, can't get the skin off? Wait, you're holding the peeler backwards. Didn't you notice?
No.
Gavin peeled the potatoes.
I can't believe how Trump courts North Korea, Gavin said.
Remind me about that, said Lorraine.
What do you mean, remind you? It's been all over the papers.
Gavin was mildly concerned but chalked it up to aging. Happens to all of us, he thought.
But Gavin noticed other things that worried him.
Lorraine, what is the rake doing in the bathroom?
There are five cartons of butter in the fridge.
Lorraine, it's freezing out. Why is the back door wide open?
The stove is on. Are you planning to bake something?
Gavin began doing the grocery shopping and cooking. He locked the doors at night and made certain all the lights were turned off.
Lorraine was tired. During all these years, she had managed a full-time job, food purchases and cooking, home and cottage maintenance and vacation planning. She drove her three sons to activities, listened to their worries, organized doctors, dentists, camp, soccer, basketball and sleepovers.

Lorraine had observed older couples where one of them was helpless. That person was fed, bathed, dressed and taken for outings. Nothing was expected from them. It seemed like such an easy way to avoid responsibility—fake Alzheimer's.

Lorraine recalled the conversation she and Gavin had before they married.

I'm not very domestic, she remembered saying. She knew the statistics. Women do a greater share of the housework and child rearing. She worried that the emotional load might be staggering, not knowing at that point, that it could also be sustaining.

Don't worry. I'll help with the meals and cleaning. It will be a fifty/fifty partnership, was Gavin's reply. They both believed it at the time.

I'm not certain I'm cut out for motherhood but I think family life could be very rewarding.

I really want to be a father. I'll take on a lot of the responsibility of raising the children.

Their first date was a Chopin concert and during the intermission she moved in close to him while he leaned against a wall. They used words like sublime and transcendent to describe the music, words they were to repeat many times over the years when making love.

There was nothing false in their complete attraction to each other. Gavin was trained in manners. Lorraine refused politeness. She tested him with this, to see how far she could go, how much he could take. He took it like a gentleman. When she pretended to lose her words, her memory of things, it was simply another kind of test, she thought.

She loved her sons. This was simply true. Robert was an actuary and only wanted to talk statistics. She feigned interest in mortality tables and probabilities, but actually found this morbid. Her middle son, Stephen, was having financial difficulties after his divorce. She and Gavin helped bail him out with some of their retirement money. His ex-wife had custody of the four children and she often called Lorraine, asking her to pitch in with the babysitting. Lorraine loved her grandchildren. This was entirely authentic as were the hugs, the games she played with them, the stories she read, bath time. Her youngest son, Brian, lived in another city and was a foreign correspondent. The couple of times she saw him were highlights in her year.

Gavin promised to help out more when he was retired. They both believed it.

The chimney fell down. The storm door didn't close, paint was peeling on the kitchen ceiling, the downstairs toilet was broken and the floorboards had gone grey with wear. Gavin didn't notice. Lorraine did.

Gavin had always been like a cheerful houseguest, waiting for his supper, reading the paper, surfing the computer or watching TV most evenings. On the weekends, he was often away on car rallies with his friend, Peter. Lists did not work. Nagging and shouting only made her feel bad and upset the children. So she went quietly through the days. Yet she understood his sincerity. He wanted her, cared for her when she was ill, worried when she was late.

Lorraine began shredding tissues and leaving them on the sofa, a chair, the side table.

I think you need to brush your teeth and have a shower, darling. You're getting a bit ripe, Lorraine.

Gavin, can you help me turn the faucet to the right setting? I'm only getting cold water.

Do I need a coat, Gavin?

Of course, can't you see it's snowing?

Where have you been, Lorraine? I was expecting you home three hours ago.

Were you? I was just driving around.

Gavin made an appointment with their GP.

Doctor Small was a kindly, by the book practitioner and told Lorraine that he would set up an appointment with a gerontologist to take the Mini-mental state assessment. Lorraine downloaded it from the internet and studied it carefully. She would have to score 19 in order not to get a CT scan or drugs at this stage.

Then she realized she might lose her driver's licence and access to the grandchildren. She had stupidly and impulsively gone through with this charade after an intense bout of self-pity.

She hadn't indulged in such thoughtless behavior since she was young. In the late 1960s and early 1970s she had taken up the rebellious stance of her generation and delayed the responsibilities of an adult life. For a long time, she wanted her freedom and a bohemian lifestyle.

When she met Gavin, she questioned her previous choices. He lived a conventional life, but this seemed more appealing to Lorraine as she faced middle-age. It wasn't a matter of settling. Gavin was handsome and brilliant.

Lorraine wondered how she was going to tell him. She wondered when would be best. Fortunately, Gavin hadn't yet voiced his concerns about her to their sons. There would be no easy way to approach this. She decided to confess when they were out for dinner one evening at a local restaurant that served Thai fusion. She felt it would be better to bring the subject up in a public place, not because Gavin hated to cause a scene in front of others, but because she thought she'd have to maintain some semblance of emotional control over her own guilt. In a neutral setting where someone on her street might walk in at any time, Lorraine believed she would have to behave like a rational person rather than the lunatic that Gavin might judge was sitting across from him.

Lorraine called him darling.

Darling, I've got something to explain to you and you're not going to like it.

What? You booked a vacation for a month in Antarctica without asking me?

No, it's way worse than that. I faked having Alzheimer's, she blurted out.

You're just scared and in denial. I'll help you. Really, I'll be there for you.

I'm not joking. I put on an act. I can prove it to you. If you give me the mental assessment test, I'll score near perfect. I already tried it on the computer.

Gavin had been completely fooled. He had lived with her long enough to know every nuance of her intimately. Yet he hadn't guessed that she had been lying. He glanced at her and realized that now, she was definitely telling the truth. Gavin twirled his hair, something he only did when he was very nervous.

I believe I participated fully in our life together. I know I enjoyed so much of it, Gavin. But sometimes I felt like a performer who needed to be fed the lines, shown the marks. I'm wondering if this dilemma is part of being a woman today—finding a role and sticking with it? I mean, Alzheimer's is a pathological inability to follow the script, right? The failure to fake it in any way at all.

Gavin stood up and walked out of the restaurant. She realized there was no possible way to excuse her behaviour that would have been meaningful to him. She smiled nervously at the waitress who brought over the bill.

Lorraine walked block after block. At best, she had hoped, this would have opened up a discussion between them. Instead, it cut the relationship dead. She was counting on his generosity but understood a line had been crossed. He was much more vulnerable now that he was older. It was when men realized how much they needed their wives. A part of Lorraine wanted to go to him. It would take a supreme effort to reconcile, but perhaps it was still possible. She knew the longer she walked, the more time he had to pack up and leave. And in various circumstances during her marriage, when she was most angry, isn't this what she had wanted?

She was on their street, close enough to their house to see that no lights were on. Lorraine went in. It was quiet and then she heard his voice. *Is that you, Lorraine? Were you out?*

Yes, of course. Don't you remember I said I was going for a long walk?

I must have dozed off. Where did you walk to?

I walked through a story but I didn't like the ending.

Why not?

We weren't in love.

I'm not tired, Lorraine.

You've been sleeping.

Were you out?

Only for a little while.

GRAND CANYON TOUR

It was almost dusk when they arrived at the Canyon and rather than following Andrea's usual plan of checking into the hotel first, they went immediately to the site which was efficiently organized for traffic. After parking the car, they walked a path to the edge.

Andrea had planned the trip to Arizona as meticulously as always. She knew exact times and dates, names of hotels and their amenities, check-in and check-out times, car rental rates and air-fare deals. She read *Frommer's* and *Fodor's* and sections of *Lonely Planet*, studied maps both print and on the internet and viewed Google images to determine what places she might want to see or not. All this preparation spoiled nothing. The trips she had taken with Greg, her husband, and Sylvia, their child, had all been splendid.

Andrea had been anxious about heights and steep drops. She wasn't certain she would be comfortable looking over. But there was an adequate wall at this starting point and she stepped confidently towards the viewing platform. She knew the canyon was grand but nothing prepared her for the immensity and spectacular vista that awaited her. She didn't know where to rest her gaze. Her family stood staring for a while then walked a ways along the rim. But it was getting dark and tomorrow morning they were leaving early for a private tour with an experienced guide.

The guide picked them up in a small van. He worked for a company that had an unpretentious marketing approach on the web which attracted her. *Hi, I'm Len,* he introduced himself. Andrea had a few minutes to study him as he opened the doors and helped them get settled. First impressions: Len was her age, that is to say, older with greying hair and creased face, moderately tall, wire-rimmed glasses, lean body, clean, pressed cords, and a crisp, blue shirt. Sexy.

He drove them away from the visitor center towards an area with fewer tourists. They pulled up to Point Imperial, and as they got out of the van, Andrea mentioned her fears. Len said it wasn't a problem. There was no wall so the scenery was visible even from a distance back. He pulled out some aluminum folding chairs and set them up.

Andrea tested her nerve. *I can go closer,* she realized.

Okay, how about this? He moved the chairs forward.

Yes, this is good. I'm comfortable here.

You're not so bad, he assured her. *Lots of people need to be farther away.*

Greg and Sylvia complimented Andrea on her newfound bravery. They were all thrilled by the view of the Painted Desert and Marble Canyon.

Len went back to the van and returned carrying a stack of Tupperware containers. He began to talk about the Canyon, its Precambrian layers of red and black rock, its geological beginnings, carved from the Colorado River, the strata of sandstone, granite, quartz, basalt and limestone. He explained how the colours came to be, the shapes, statistics on age and depth.

Two billion years ago the layers of igneous and metamorphic rocks formed. Above this are layers and layers of sedimentary rocks.

Then Len spoke about the canyon in an intimate way, perhaps testing them to see if they were the kind of travellers he thought they might be.

When I was young, I hiked into the canyon many times, camped out overnight, saw the stars. It always seemed like a trip from the past into the future. Kind of an eerie feeling.

He paused after telling them. Was he gauging their reaction? Only Andrea commented, *how important this place is for you!*

Len proceeded to open the containers one at a time, handing over the small rock samples for the family to examine and hold. Sylvia, fascinated by every detail, raised her hand as if she were in school to ask questions. He nodded at her to go ahead, answered each one carefully. Greg had more technical queries about bio-chemistry and geophysics. Len was knowledgeable, could engage with this.

After about an hour, everyone got back in the van. They were on their way to Cape Royal and the view of the natural arch, Angel's Window, which framed the Colorado River. Along the way Len pointed out mule deer that were grazing near a wooded area and said there were lots of other animals too like bobcats, coyote and skunks. He said hundreds of birds flew in the vicinity including Dark Eyed Juncos, the Yuma Clapper Rail and California Condor. He handed Sylvia a book filled with identifying photographs.

The plan was to continue on to the Indian reservation. Len said the Indians didn't like to be called Natives. The Navajo tribe ran a restaurant and gift shop in a huge wooden building. Len was known to the owners, who greeted him, and sat everyone at a large round table. The food was mainly American or Mexican fare, burgers and enchiladas but fry bread was on the menu.

Len must have realized they were an introverted family who talked sparely, so Andrea saw that he took the initiative as a host, and began telling them something about himself.

I was born in Prescott, one of six kids. My draft number was six. I learned a lot in the Marines but was lucky not to go to 'Nam. I lived in New Hampshire for a while, worked at the post office.

Andrea asked him if he'd read Bukowski's book but he hadn't. *I missed the Canyon. One of my brothers set up this tour company so I moved back.*

Sylvia said she was already too full to finish her meal. Len assured her it didn't matter. *My mother had a saying, Do your best and leave the rest.*

I play fiddle in a band in the summer, bluegrass mostly, Len continued. *But I really like listening to Early music.*

Greg, whose preference was classical, joined in the conversation. *I play the flute, Bach is my all-time favourite composer.* Andrea added, *I love the baroque, but bluegrass too.*

One of the waiters resembled Warren Beatty. Andrea felt compelled to make a dumb joke about the actor. It was her physical attraction to Len that made her think of the joke. Len laughed even though it was lame and not the right setting for this kind of humour, but Greg didn't know who Warren Beatty was. She loved him for that.

After lunch, Len told them they could browse in the store for a while before moving on. The rugs, pottery and jewelry were advertised as authentic but many of the items had a knick-knack quality and an assembly line aesthetic. Within a few minutes Greg and Andrea asked if there was anywhere nearby they could go instead.

I can take you to see the petrified logs. There are some in the desert close by. They come from trees that were uprooted millions of years ago and carried 400 miles.

It was a short drive. When they got out of the van, Andrea felt like an alien invader as if she were trespassing in this barren landscape. Greg kept repeating the vast numbers and Sylvia hugged Andrea hard around the waist. They gathered small pieces of stone.

I'd like to stop at a local Indian market by the Little Colorado, Len suggested.

Andrea, aware that this community survived on visitors' dollars, said okay. They pulled up to a roadside clearing where there were a couple of long tables and a few Indians sitting at them. The tables were covered in hand-made crafts, mostly beads but some metal work as well. There were only a couple of other people browsing. Len checked out the goods and then came up close to Andrea. He held out his wrist. He was wearing a rope bracelet studded with juniper seeds. *Very masculine*, Andrea said.

She didn't really want to buy anything. Greg only wore a watch and Sylvia earrings. When she was younger, Andrea had quite a collection of folk-art necklaces, but got out of the habit of wearing them when she was breast-feeding Sylvia, who constantly tugged at them. She purchased a turquoise necklace.

When they got back on the road, Len said it was the end of the tour. Andrea imagined how he lived—definitely in a cabin with open plank shelves filled with books, CDs and some smaller tools. There would be a wall of salvaged, sash windows opening onto a view of the forest and Bill Williams Mountain. Len reminded her of men she had once known, men who had a passion for something. They had a looseness that came with counter-cultural experimentation, popular when she was young. Greg had his passions too, but he and Andrea were older when they married, ready for a more conventional family life. They set parts of themselves aside, she more than him. Greg sometimes kissed her when he didn't want sex. Andrea could count the number of times he told her he loved her, so she knew it was sincere.

With that old style of yearning, she wanted Len. Tears came to her eyes at the idea of parting. She was wearing sunglasses so Greg didn't notice. Len parked the van and stood with them for a while at Mather Point. They took a last look at the cliffs changing colour with the movement of the sun.

These cycles of the earth, the ancient rotation of our world, make death less of a threat, said Len.

We're not that old yet, Greg said, taking Sylvia's hand and putting his arm around Andrea. She smiled at Greg and removed her sunglasses, as the daylight glare subsided.

GREAT SALT LAKE

Richard's independence was sometimes understood as lack of need. Long days spent on the shores of Great Salt Lake, or in the lab, were seen as his desire for solitude—his devotion to brine shrimp, an eccentricity. Occasionally, some of the Mormon boys from Lake Point, would venture near and ask him what he was doing. He eagerly pulled in a net—showing off hundreds of shrimp, explaining that their ancestors lived over five million years ago in the Mediterranean, that the eggs or cysts could go metabolically dormant for two years if conditions weren't right for hatching, that until maturity they had a single eye called the naupliar, which then later developed into the compound eyes on two stalks.

When he saw the boys' attention wavering to the pelicans, cormorants or diving terns he told them how cysts were sent with the astronauts into the cosmic rays of space, and how ninety per cent of the embryos died. He told them there were over one hundred billion brine flies at the lake, eaten by the birds. It held the boys' interest for a minute or two more, before they hopped on their bikes and headed towards the town. At the end of the day, he sometimes drove into that town for gas at the Texaco or a quick bite from one of the fast food outlets. Sometimes, he saw those same boys in their white shirts and black pants crowding around the doors of the Latter Day Saints chapel.

★

Richard had been shunted around to foster homes since shortly after he was born. He didn't like to talk about, or think back on these experiences. He ran off from his last placement when the abuse became unbearable. He was only fifteen. He hitchhiked across the country, picking up dishwashing jobs or farm work where he could.

★

It took twenty-two minutes to drive from Salt Lake City to Great Salt Lake State Park. Richard spent most of his weekends there looking through a portable microscope at the bacteria that digest dead brine shrimp and brine flies. The bacteria gave the water a reddish tint at the end of the growing season. Richard, who was concerned about environmental issues, knew the lake contained close to five billion tons of salt. Even with the mining of salts for sodium chloride and cattle licks, the supply would never run out. Minerals poured in from mountain rivers and streams but there was no outlet. The eggs of the brine shrimp were harvested to feed Asian prawns.

During the week, Richard worked in an assay lab testing for the heavy metals that had to be extracted from the nutritional supplements manufactured by Utah Health Salts Inc. Richard had found a job as a stock boy at Utah Health. It was a small, family owned company and after a few years, the proprietor, Mr. Donaldson, recognized Richard's potential. He encouraged him to take night courses and get his high school diploma. Then he helped with scholarship applications and Richard entered the undergraduate science program as a part-time mature student at the University of Utah. After Richard completed his studies, Mr. Donaldson promoted him to lab technician.

Richard liked where he lived. There was a small black population in the city and he rented a room in Rose Park, from the Turners who had two young children. He was included in Thanksgiving. Christmas and Easter dinners as well as backyard BBQs, where he was referred to as Uncle Rick. He had dated a few of the fine women in his community. His longest relationship was with Mira, a nurse at the Shriners Hospital. He thought he loved her, but when she asked for a commitment after seven months, he broke it off, telling her he wasn't ready for marriage.

★

There was a small café with an outdoor patio within walking distance of the university where Richard enjoyed sipping an iced coffee and reading the paper. It was at this café where Iris first took notice of him. He was tall, dark and handsome. She laughed at the cliché of her assessment. He looked up and realized a very pretty young woman was staring at him.

Hi, do you live in Salt Lake?

I do.

I'm Iris. I was hoping to meet someone local, to get to know the area. I'm here for the summer, working as an instructor at the university. At this point, she lifted her cup, brought it to his table, and sat down.

I just came from Colorado where I completed my Ph.D. I didn't want to leave Boulder but I couldn't get work there. I really like hiking. Can you recommend any trails? What's your name by the way?

Richard, he replied.

There are plenty of trails a short drive from downtown. Dry Gulch, Peach Grove Jack's Peak. They all have great views. Some are pretty rocky but the trails are well marked.

Richard decided not to tell her about Antelope Island. He had spent many summer vacations there. All he needed was a small tent, bathing suit, and a supply of food. He liked to float in the bay watching the gulls overhead and then the sunset. Afterward he stretched out on the sand, the white oolitic grains like pearls. He knew the brine flies don't bite or land on people. Richard had hiked almost everywhere on the island and saw antelopes, bison, coyotes, deer and bighorn sheep roaming the wetlands, grasslands and mountains.

I'd really like to hike with you sometime. Maybe you could be my guide?

I'm pretty busy, he hedged.

What do you do?

He told her briefly about his lab work.

I'm in computers. I'm teaching programming to undergraduates.

Richard took note of how Iris had the same pale skin and light hair as his last foster mother. An image of the brine shrimp passed through his mind—their golden, feathery bodies. He could observe them for hours in the water or fixed under the microscope. He studied every detail, every angle.

Iris tried to keep the conversation going. *So, what was it like growing up in Salt Lake? The scenery alone is so stunning.*

Richard remained silent.

Did your parents take you for a hike very often?

Richard smiled at the unintended metaphors. He resisted the urge to invite himself back to her place and fuck her. He pushed his chair away from the table, picked up his paper, nodded curtly and turned into the street.

INTERMISSION

INTRODUCTION

They drove in that time between day and darkness when the Ontario sky glows with an eerie light. Eileen and Jasper had planned this trip to Stratford weeks ago. Although they were both English scholars, neither specialized in Elizabethan literature. Jasper's area was medieval and Eileen's the Canadian novel. Despite her Ph.D., Eileen was only able to get a lecturer's position at her university while Jasper had full tenure. Eileen was slightly resentful. She was ambitious and believed she too would have a professorship eventually.

They had a brief debate about whether to see Lear again but as per Jasper's preference, they purchased tickets for *Love's Labour's Lost*. Neither had read or seen the work in years although both remembered that the king of Navarre was the main character and that he and his lords made a vow to renounce women for several years. It was an oath they could not keep.

Jasper and Eileen had met eight months ago and the relationship deepened. Their interests were compatible and Jasper was suave and attractive. Eileen understood he might be ready for a commitment. When they were considering the weekend in Stratford, Jasper mentioned that his father had proposed to his mother there.

It was dark when they arrived. The Globe B&B was near the main street in the oldest part of town, where many of the mansions had been converted into inns. They stepped onto a wide verandah lit with a lantern-shaped porch light and rang the doorbell. A middle-aged man wearing a cardigan and corduroys opened the door and introduced himself as John. He was expecting them.

Welcome. Come right in. Can I help you with your bag? he asked Eileen, as he took it from her. *Your room is right up this way,* and he led them through a charming vestibule and up a wooden staircase with an intricately carved newel post. On the landing, they passed a Victorian stained glass window with a floral design. Their bedroom and attached bath was at the end of the hallway on the second floor.

Here you go then, said John. *I'm sure you'll be very comfortable. Breakfast is served at 8:30.*

Their room was cozy and quaint. There were a couple of landscapes on the walls, a high dresser and an antique nightstand topped by a porcelain ewer and bowl. Eileen was taken with the brass bed and patchwork quilt. Jasper admired the well uphol- stered rocker and immediately sat in it while Eileen unpacked, undressed and slipped into her nightgown. She had brought sev- eral books of poetry and the plan was to read aloud to Jasper who enjoyed the timbre of her voice. Eileen got into bed and opened Anne Carson's *The Beauty of the Husband.* Jasper took off his clothes and joined her. He always slept nude. Jasper massaged Eileen's thigh while she read and she only got through two poems before passion overcame them and the book was flung on the floor.

*

They had not pulled the shade and the morning sun woke them early. Jasper ran a hot bath in the large, claw footed tub and they made love again while it filled. Since it was well before 8:30 they lingered in the warmth of the water sitting at opposite ends, their legs intertwined.

John enjoyed baking and there were scones with raspberry jam for breakfast. The coffee was freshly roasted from a bean that John said was from Africa. Eileen and Jasper had the morning ahead of them and decided to walk through the park along the Avon River. The swans had been released from their winter barn and were floating on the small current that carried them down- stream. It was an idyllic scene and Eileen noticed that Jasper was lost in thought. Perhaps he was thinking ahead to the evening meal that would follow the matinee performance. Reservations had been made for the restaurant in the converted church. Did he have a ring for her?

They arrived at the Shakespeare gardens and crossed the double-arch stone bridge and back. They rested on a bench in the pergola and then explored the flower beds bordered by thrift and boxwood in the parterre.

So let me show you around, Eileen playfully adopted a tour guide's cadence. *Here we have roses and peonies,* she began with the easy to identify.

Of course, I know these flowers, Jasper said, slightly offended.

Yes—but what about these? and she pointed to the cowslip, then the hyssop and eryngium, none of which Jasper knew the names of.

And now for the grand finale! she teased. *These magenta beauties are corncockle.*

What the heck is corncockle and how on earth do you know this?

Corncockle is considered a weed in wheat fields. And I confess, I researched these gardens before I came.

Jasper laughed and kissed her, delighted by her ability to entertain him.

★

As it was getting near lunch, they headed along Downie Street to George where *Raja* was located. Jasper was enthusiastic about all types of Asian food. He ordered the King Prawn Masala and Eileen chose the Lamb Korma. They lingered over their meal enjoying the ambience of crisp white table cloths and ornate chandeliers.

I'm thinking we could travel to Asia sometime, Jasper ventured. *Southeast Asia, I mean.*

I'd be interested in doing that, Eileen kept her tone even. Could he be thinking of a honeymoon trip?

★

After lunch, they headed to the theater. The trumpets were already blaring when they arrived, signaling that it was time for people to take their seats. As they were sitting down, Eileen heard Jasper's name being called. He turned to see who it was.

Lahn. Hello. Jasper greeted a lovely Vietnamese woman sitting just across the aisle from them.

Jasper. It's great to see you. I'm here with my aunt. Let's catch up at the intermission.

Distracted, Eileen had difficulty focusing on the performance. She was tempted but refrained from grasping Jasper's hand for ballast. Certain lines jumped out at her and became a refrain in her mind: Love is familiar. Love is a devil. Vows are but breath, and breath a vapor is.

When Act III concluded and the house lights came up, Jasper sprang out of his seat as did Lahn, and they hugged. The elderly aunt nodded as Eileen trailed after Jasper.

Eileen, I'd like you to meet Lahn, Jasper introduced them and they made their way to the lobby, Jasper and Lahn leading. From behind Eileen could see the straight fall to the waist of Lahn's exquisite black hair.

They stood near the bar and Jasper suggested drinks but both women declined. Eileen was dismayed by how intimidated she felt by Lahn's beauty. She was very slim with ivory skin and was wearing some form of traditional clothing that involved a silk tunic and trousers. It had been years since Eileen felt self-conscious about her own body. She had come to terms with being tall. The phrase "large boned" had gone out of fashion and she hadn't thought of it in ages. But it came to mind now. Eileen reminded herself that her best features were her honey coloured hair and sea green eyes.

So Jasper. What have you been up to? Lahn asked him as she touched his arm.

I'm a professor at the University of Toronto and I've just published a book with a new slant on the Canterbury Tales, but I won't bore you with the details.

Yes, Eileen interjected. *He's got me to bore. Right, darling?*

Jasper ignored the remark and Eileen was embarrassed that she'd resorted to sarcasm.

Lahn said, touching his arm again, *That's really impressive, Jasper. How many books is it now? I remember three from before.*

Yup. This one's the fourth.

What before? Eileen wanted to ask but kept silent.

So what about you, Lahn. Are you still dancing?

Yes. But I'm not with the Gilman troupe anymore. I was recruited by Toronto Associated Dance. It's kind of a big deal. And they're giving me solos. So I'm pretty pumped about this.

And how's Mark doing?

I'm not with him anymore. We had a bad breakup and I'm still recovering from it.

Lahn turned to Eileen. *How long have you known Jasper?*

We've been together since November.

And what line of work are you in?

I'm a lecturer in the English department at Ryerson and I've just finished my Ph.D. So Jasper and I have a lot in common, I mean both of us being academics. I've just had a book published as well. It was my thesis about Julia Beckwith. She was from the Maritimes and nobody has heard of her, but in 1824 her book, St. Ursula's Convent, was the first novel published in Canada.

Okay. Can't say I'm going to be reading that one, or any of yours, Jasper, for that matter, Lahn smiled. *I'm more of the contemporary best-seller type.*

Not one to minimize her accomplishments, however, recondite, and sensing there was something at stake here Eileen said, *Yes, I'm not surprised.*

Lahn countered with, *By the way, I'm launching a clothing line. It's been picked up by one of the boutiques on Queen Street. I doubt my designs are your style though, Eileen.*

Eileen had to pee. She excused herself and said she'd meet Jasper back in the theater. The line for the washroom was long even though the intermission was almost over. Most of the women were older which was expected for a matinee. In pantsuits and costume jewellery, they dutifully waited for their turn on the toilets. There were a couple of younger women in interesting getups that involved wide skirts, small sweaters and coloured ankle socks.

The line moved briskly so Eileen was able to return to the theater just as the lights were dimming for the fourth act. When she reached her seat, Lahn was sitting in it. Jasper shrugged and

made a sad face then pointed to the empty seat beside the old
aunt.

Completely ruffled and distracted now, Eileen was only able
to seize on lines that spoke to her situation: *Love whose month is
ever May, Spied a blossom passing fair, Playing in the wanton air.*

But in Act V, she found courage in the speech, *Arm wenches
arm! Encounters mounted are against your peace.* She still had some
fight left in her and would not give up easily.

After the final bows and applause, they all met in the aisle.

*Eileen and I were thinking of grabbing a bite to eat. Would you and
your aunt like to join us?*

What do you think, Auntie? We're in no rush to get home, right?

The aunt nodded her assent and so it was set that they would
share a meal.

★

A green lawn, spread before them as they exited the theater.
Girlishly, Lahn leapt into the air, showing off a Batterie and
Double Cabriole. *It's such a glorious day,* she laughed, and Jasper
laughed with her.

Lahn dashed around encouraging Jasper to try a jump as well.
He tripped just as he was lifting off the ground and fell against
Lahn knocking her down. *Oh my God, I'm very sorry,* Jasper apol-
ogized. *I'm so clumsy.*

Eileen could see he was completely mortified by this loss of
dignity.

My ankle. It's broken! I'm sure it's broken! Lahn wailed as the
old aunt and Eileen rushed over to assist her. Jasper seemed dazed
and hadn't gotten to his feet yet. Lahn was calming down and
tried to stand. As she walked back and forth, she realized her
ankle was only slightly sprained.

Jasper was up and uninjured. He linked his arm with Eileen's
and kissed her. *You are the best wench I've ever met.* Eileen smiled
but made no reply. They walked hand in hand to the restaurant
in front of Lahn and her aunt. Jasper did not turn around or look
back.

POOL

On her 70th birthday Carol gave herself the gift of a Caribbean vacation. She chose the island furthest south, the hottest, the one with lava cliffs dropping into the ocean. In the photos on the internet she was attracted to the hotel with the large T-shaped pool and booked a single. She also liked that the resort seemed close to an urban center. But she neglected to convert kilometers to miles, and once there, discovered that it was a forty minute walk into the town of Willemstad.

Carol spent the first day mostly swimming. It wasn't busy at the pool, but she was disappointed by the fact that on each side, stairways of six to eight steps extended underwater and shortened the lap lengths. A young redhead sunning herself on a lounger reminded Carol of her long ago self, when she first met her husband. Their difficult marriage finally fell apart and Carol had been alone for close to twenty years. She occasionally thought about searching for a new partner but at her age, it might mean tucks, fillers, lifts and dyes, even to attract an old codger. Screw that.

On the second morning, Carol decided to walk into town. She found a narrow, paved road adjacent to the sea and set out. A picturesque row of fishing shanties lined the beach for several miles while a strong wind from the water kept her cool. It was an isolated road with only an occasional car passing. After a few miles, she encountered an industrial area with a chain link, barbed wire fence, beyond which towered a series of oil tanks on the Shell property. This soon ended in a park-like section which had a memorial made of piled stones to commemorate the deaths of unnamed slaves.

The road ended on the outskirts of Willemstad and she was forced along a busy highway-like stretch, lined with auto repair shops, tin huts and shoddily constructed, cheap motels. Nobody seemed to be around although there was a steady stream of traffic.

She observed that on the other side of the roadway there was a pleasant looking brick path, shaded with acacia trees. Carol crossed over. For a brief moment, she enjoyed the play of light through the leaves but soon the stench of a massive cesspool, where the ten storey cruise ships dumped their raw sewage, assaulted her.

After a few more blocks she came to the Otrobanda quarter and walked along De Rouvilleweg where vendors were selling manufactured wooden masks, scarves and drums. She wondered if they were made in China. A short distance further brought her to the Queen Emma, a hinged bridge that crossed St. Anna Bay into Punda. The bridge was open to allow a ship through and she waited in a small crowd of tourists until it closed and pedestrians were allowed to cross over. The shoreline in Punda was lined with Dutch colonial style buildings painted in tropical green, pink and yellow.

The streets of Willemstad were filled with walkers, interesting shops and cafes and she planned to come back every day to explore the city, but now she was getting tired. The sun was high and hot. Carol was ready for a swim, so she grabbed a taxi back to the hotel.

Almost every lounge chair was taken. A father and his two sons were stationed on three sides of the pool throwing a nerf ball back and forth, and obstructing the pathway that Carol needed to swim her laps. She began an aggressive breast stroke past the area where the father was standing and after a few times back and forth, he moved a slight distance away from the side of the pool, leaving her a narrow lane. She had been lucky on other vacations where the pools were almost empty, people only dipping in occasionally, to cool down from sunbathing. Nevertheless, the effort of the swim released her nervous tension and she felt relaxed as she lay on her towel drying off in the heat.

She ate dinner early, as was her habit, at the pool-side restaurant. A few families with very young children were also eating at that time. She enjoyed eavesdropping on their conversations, mostly the parents giving instructions on what to choose from the menu or how to behave properly at the table. The girls were in crisp, pastel sundresses, the boys in striped, linen shorts and the kind of dressy casual shirts seen on royal children.

After the meal, Carol went up the grand staircase that culminated in a waterfall. She checked out the balcony by the lobby and decided this was where she would spend her evenings. There were comfortable couches, a view to the beach and a wonderful breeze weaving through the palms. She played a few word games on her iPhone and then read until bedtime. Her ground floor room looked out on a modest hedge of lemon vines beyond which was the sea. She slept well.

The hotel offered several tours to different parts of the island and Carol chose the Shete Boka Park excursion. It was leaving after lunch but the bus was air conditioned and the park was by the water so she expected to be comfortable. She would try a morning swim, hoping that the father and his boys would keep to their afternoon schedule. There were definitely fewer guests, however the game of catch was in full play. She watched them for a while. The father was a good looking man of about forty. He had thick dark hair, a muscular body with biceps and an old-style heart tattoo on one. The younger boy appeared to be about ten and still had baby fat. The older boy, whom Carol guessed to be around fourteen, was lean and muscular like his dad. He wore a shiny gold cross on a short chain around his neck and had a confident swagger. Carol slid into the water. She started her laps and the father made space for her again. She was resigned to the slap of the wet ball as it went from hand to hand.

The bus stopped in the Boka Tabla area of Shete Park. The trail was along high lava hills with a sublime view of lavish waves rolling in from the turquoise sea and cresting white on the rocks. It was almost too magnificent. Carol resisted the urge to take off her sandals and step barefoot on the cutting scoria.

They were there the next morning. This time the wife and mother was with them, a gorgeous brunette with a deep tan. Her wavy, well cut hair was shoulder-length and she had on a white bikini that revealed her full breasts, firm belly and long legs. Her tattoo was just above the band of the bathing suit bottom and was a lily. For a full hour, she did not leave the lounger, her boys taking breaks from time to time from the ball game to sit with her, perched on the edge of the narrow cot. Occasionally, she sat up to smooth down the hair of the younger boy or apply more sunscreen to the back of the older one. The father acknowledged Carol as she went into the water, so she asked where he was from. New Jersey.

Curacao had its history of brutality. Slaves arrived in the 17th century but the lava beds precluded plantations. Instead, the half dead Africans who came off the ships were fattened up and allowed to regain their health for a year before being sent off to islands more hospitable to cultivation. Carol learned this at the Kura Hulanda museum. Room after horrifying room revealed terrible cruelty, torture and suffering. She needed to see this. The children wrenched from their mothers. Her own child dead in his crib after two months. It was on a different scale, but excruciating, even now, even years and years later.

Carol spent her last vacation day at the pool. A new group of middle-aged tourists from the American mid-west had arrived and were standing on the steps partway into the water discussing the best places to eat in Willemstad. The father and his boys were there, of course, and Carol felt particularly irritated. It was obnoxious how perfect this family was: so attractive, clearly affectionate and loving. Carol started her laps. The father actually spoke to her, complimented her on her discipline and stamina. The ball hit her cheek. Carol caught it and swam with it to the far end of the pool. Across the way, the younger boy held out his hands for her to throw it to him. She stood holding the ball. He reached out again and said please. She smiled and he smiled believing the teasing to be over. He held out his hands again. She couldn't let it go.

POVERTY DAY

Aman in tight khakis, black t-shirt, black loafers, no socks introduces himself to me as Clark. He's smooth shaven and has a full head of hair that is well trimmed. I notice because it was a look I cultivated at one time. They choose people like me, educated but down on their luck from some flaw. Mine was embarrassingly banal. Alcohol. Got hooked on booze and couldn't shake it. I had a good education and made it into university, just before they closed the doors to anyone who couldn't afford one hundred thousand a year for tuition.

You don't mind if I rip your coat along this seam, do you, Andrew? Clark has scissors in his hand and without waiting for my answer, snips into the sleeve and then with both hands, grabs the fabric and tears. He steps back to examine the effect, and satisfied, puts the scissors on his work table. I catch a glimpse of myself in the mirror. I'm startled to see how bald I've become. My head is shiny and my face is red from scratches I got trying to shave with a piece of broken glass. Patches of beard along my chin make me realize I didn't do a very good job.

You're too clean! Clark seems disappointed. He picks up a jar of dirt and approaches me. *Need a little on your forehead and hands. Stick your fingers in and twirl them around.* Clark doesn't seem interested in how I wash but I tell him.

In the warmer weather I swim in the East River after dark.

We aren't allowed in the water during the day, but I've come to appreciate being in the river at night. When the sky is clear and the stars are sharp overhead, I can recover those feelings of appreciation that I felt in my previous life.

In the winter, I tell, Clark, *the Privation Police come around with basins of hot water and old towels donated by the residents of the Upper West side. They don't want us spreading disease so they let us have a sponge bath in a lobby or over a heating vent. There's a gauge they use to measure how much we stink. Anything over six and we qualify.*

Clark laughs. *This is news to me, man. I didn't realize they actually keep tabs on your hygiene.*

There's plenty Clark doesn't know. We were warned not to offer any information. Clark looks me over one more time, tells me I'm ready to go on display. We walk down a passage, behind the store windows. I can see how the tableaus have been arranged. There's a real fire burning in a metal barrel with a few black guys gathered around it. When I pass by, they nod their heads towards me and wink. I've seen them plenty of times on the street. Their eyes twinkle a bit in the glare as they joke around and restlessly move their bodies to the sound of a rap song. They seem to be trying to project the idea of down but not out.

In the next window, an older woman pushes a shopping cart back and forth from one wall to the other. The cart is loaded with junk like a broken toaster, unravelled sweater, torn pink plastic raincoat, inside-out umbrella and shoes with holes in their soles. The woman has a mangy, pet cat she pulls along on a leash. It yowls and hisses in protest. Clark nods at her in approval. *Good work, Angie, you remembered not to wear underpants? Don't forget to lift your skirt once in a while. Gives them a thrill and gets people hanging around the store longer so they don't miss the show. Just remember it's a flash, not up for more than a second.*

I am in the third window. Clark gives me a pep talk and goes over my routine. *You're going to do fine. Make sure you drink all the wine. Get to the finish line but pace yourself. Not too much at once.* I glance at the four wine bottles already in place. A couple of open, empty ones are strewn around for atmosphere. *It's okay if you vomit but not too close to the window. We don't want to scare away the customers.* One word flashes neon green above me on the sign hanging from the ceiling: WINO.

Ever since the government got rid of the Human Rights Commission, anything is acceptable. The idea is to make people feel good about themselves by humiliating others. It's the concept behind Poverty Day. Put the losers on show as exotics. Before the big sweep, you saw the disabled, people of colour, and the impoverished anywhere in the city. That's all changed. They've designated the Bowery as a kind of living museum. The homeless are allowed to live rough in an area of about seven blocks. Even though I'm out on the street, I consider myself one of the lucky ones. Rumour is that apart from about 150 people, anyone who was destitute got shipped out or worse, right after democracy failed. I heard that they emptied the prisons but nobody is sure what happened to the inmates. They kept on a few of us to ease the conscience of the rich. *Look,* said the TV newscasters, appointed by the President, *reports are false that only those in the top 5% are left in New York City.*

As one of the few indigents who remained, I had a briefing from the Privation Police. We could do whatever we wanted as long as a) we committed no acts of violence or theft unless it was against one of our own b) we did not bother people for a job or a place to stay c) we did not procreate. They will let us die out and the next generation of the successful, will only know about poverty from a single page in the history books.

Some unmarried police officers and soldiers are billeted in the Bowery. But most of the houses are used to store municipal equipment. We are not allowed inside. For a hefty price a few citizens can come down to our neighbourhood once in a while. It makes them feel cosmopolitan. No interaction or conversation is permitted, but visitors can take photographs.

Clark is clapping his hands to signal to us that the curtains are opening. In the street in front of me, a couple of teenage girls point at me and laugh. I'm more of a novelty to the younger generation who haven't seen anyone struggle. They have no idea what it was like when automation was phased in and the population was starving. It was around that time that I started drinking. The few of us left in financial advisory positions knew it was only a matter of time before our work would be completely absorbed by the AI department.

The number of shoppers increases as the morning wears on. Because I'm not one of the bigger draws, I'm only here until noon. Besides I'll be passed out by then. I can see a crowd gathering by Angie's window. She must have her skirt up. Suddenly I can hear what the spectators are saying. Clark, or someone, flipped a switch by mistake. The speakers that pipe music into the street at Christmas, are supposed to be off. They are two-way so that passersby can say Hi to Santa and he can say Hi back. Giggled shouts of *Gross* and *I didn't need to see that* fill the air.

By this time I'm through my first bottle and feeling pretty happy. *Hey, baby,* I call and whistle at a beautiful blonde who, despite herself, smiles. An attractive guy steps up to her and they link arms. *I feel kind of sorry for him,* she says. *Yeah, poor fuck,* he agrees and they move on. It's been years since I've heard a word of sympathy and even though I remind myself it was actually pity, I'm not prepared for how deprived I feel. I start sweating, open another bottle and wonder if I've made a mistake, maybe shouldn't have been so eager to volunteer. How could I have hoped that showing enthusiasm for a government initiative, might in some way lead to an advantage?

A group of children stop to stare at me. They are all wearing camel hair coats, brown leather boots and the boys have tweed caps, also brown. I have to admit I'm pleased, even excited to see them. There are no kids in the Bowery. *Hey guys,* I laugh and wave. They seem taken aback and nervous. *He's dumb. I hate him. What's a wino?*

I can't believe I'm tearing up. I was the oldest in my family, loved my younger brothers. I don't know what became of them. I know they were doing well in business and academia at one point but our relationship was cut off by the army. I turn my back, take a swig, line the empty bottles up and when I turn round, the kids are gone. Many people walk by and don't stop. I've forgotten how pleasure, how leisure looked. Their heads are up, shoulders relaxed, footsteps firm on the pavement.

An older man does peer in. He shakes his head, says, *You should be ashamed.* I want to argue with him, explain that before the regime change, I had started rehab. But now I'm feeling sleepy and when I begin to talk my speech is slurred. Anyway, he's quickly moved on. Two young men in suits that make them seem stiff, slow down and stop to check me out. A wave of horror washes over me. I recognize them from my old firm on Wall St. but calm down when I realize they have no idea who I am.

I've finished my third bottle and I'm bleary and bored. I blow a raspberry and stick my fingers up my nostrils.

What an asshole.

Nah, he's just an infantile screw-up.

What did you say? I roar and with renewed energy, advancing toward the window. I open my zipper and piss up and down the glass.

Christ. Let's get out of here. Wait, I think we should report him.

A minute later Clark appears, alarmed and furious. He yanks the curtains shut and when I flap my cock at him, he calls security. I hear one of the guards start to say, *He's going to be sent to*—

But before they can restrain me, Clark yells, *Fire.* A metal barrel shooting flames rolls down the back hall, followed by a frantic cat. I start opening the curtains so everyone can enjoy the show. The black guys are racing towards the exit pushing the cart with a screaming Angie inside it. I smash a bottle against the wall. *It's a special day,* I bellow. *Let's celebrate.*

Sequoia

They were a young couple when the wagon train crossed the Sierra Nevadas, Samuel only twenty and Annie nineteen. It had been a difficult journey up the steep pass and through the snowy peaks. When they arrived at the Sequoia forest early in the morning, Annie seemed captivated by the giant trees. The others in their group were eager to move quickly into the valley but Annie asked Samuel if they could spend a few hours longer among the trees. They kept two horses and Samuel said, *We'll catch up to you before evening.*

Annie was not a pious girl. She had attended church back east to please her parents and the townspeople, but could never give herself over to Christ. In this grove, however, such a sense of serenity infused her that she told Samuel, *This is a sacred place.* He felt slightly uncomfortable as Annie embraced part of one of the trunks which was so enormous Annie thought it would take a dozen people with arms outstretched to encircle it. She rested her cheek against the bark, stroked the areas she could reach and began whispering so softly to the Sequoia that Samuel could not pick up what she was saying.

Samuel held his head back to see the top of the trees. He estimated their height was around 200 feet. The rustling of their leaves made him uneasy since he could not detect any wind. To take his mind off this unsettling feeling, he called to Annie to have some lunch. They sat on the ground with their backs against her tree and Samuel took some bread and bacon from his pack. After eating, they wandered further from the trail. Annie complained that her legs ached but she did not want to rest, did not stop touching the trees. Samuel tried to make light of it by teasing. *You love them more than me. I didn't realize size was such an excitement for you.*

Annie smiled and told him to shush. *You can't compete,* she teased back and caressed Samuel playfully. Just as he was about to

kiss her, Annie collapsed on the ground. Diarrhea coursed down
her legs and vomit poured from her mouth. She started to whis-
per again, fervently as if in a fever. But when Samuel felt her
forehead she was cool. *Can you try to stand up?* He was pleading.
There was no response. She had already lost consciousness.
Samuel put her head in his lap, begged her to live. His tears fell
on her cheeks as he bent over her. She died there from the
cholera which had lurked in her body for three days.

Samuel cursed the trees. If Annie had not been so
enthralled, they would have moved on with the group and perhaps reached a doctor in time to save her. Samuel had no shovel
or spade with him. He pondered taking her body tied to the
horse. But then she would be buried in an unknown spot
among strangers. Instead Samuel left her exposed beside one of
the largest trees.

His fellow travellers on the wagon train listened to Samuel's
story of Annie's death. After months of participating in this expe-
dition, his deep love for Annie was well known and everyone
was aware of his gentle nature. Besides there was no mistaking his
grief. He would have had to have been another Joseph Jefferson
to give so convincing a performance.

Samuel settled in California and became part of a logging
crew. American showmen had the idea of cutting Sequoia trees
and exhibiting their vast trunks like sideshow freaks. It took
twenty-five men ten days to drill holes and de-stabilize a tree and
it would fall with such force that mud and stones shot one hundred feet into the air. Even more barbaric was the skinning of a
tree so that its intact bark could be displayed. Samuel was one of
the most enthusiastic of the drillers and showed tremendous
strength with a saw. He was a witness to the agony of each tree
falling. He never married and lived in the logging camps until his
death.

★

As a small boy growing up in Visalia in the 1950s, Sam went
on many hiking trips in the Sierras with his father, who was chief

of Tulare County's clinical lab and with his mother, who was an insurance adjustor with Cigna. Sam was powerfully drawn to the Sequoias and was enthusiastic when his father proposed they go camping for several weeks each summer. The thing about Sequoias was their immensity and age. Some were thousands of years old, as tall as a twenty-six storey building.

During high school, Sam volunteered as a trail labourer. He often had a sense of déjà vu which he credited to the frequency of hikes during his childhood. After graduation, he applied to and was accepted in the environmental sciences program at Berkeley. His ambition was to be a Ranger in the Calaveras Big Tree State Park.

As early as 1890, legislation was passed to save the groves. Sequoia and General Grant National Parks were established, and by 1921, the National Geographic Society had raised enough money to buy land and create the Kings Canyon National Park. But into the 1950s, Sequoias were cut down. A single Sequoia log contained more board footage than a whole acre of northern pine. One tree could supply enough fence posts to surround an eight-thousand-acre ranch. Even though the wood was dry, fine-grained and brittle, Sequoias were logged for shingles, novelty items, patio furniture and pencils. More than seventy-five per-cent of a tree might shatter when felled unless great care was taken to create a feather-bedded trench.

When Sam entered university, concern and passion for the environment was increasing. He believed he could be a leader in his field, make a difference and continue to protect the trees. Upon completion of his degree, he joined the National Park Service as a resource manager.

★

Sam caught sight of Hanna by the rail near the General Sherman tree. Lost in a kind of devotion, she wasn't aware he was watching her. It was late in the fall and few other people were around. Sam took in her patrician beauty, graceful body, tanned skin and closely cropped sun-bleached hair. He walked over.

Did you notice how barren the ground is beneath the trees? The sequoias depend on fire to clear the duff. Otherwise, the seeds won't germinate.

Hanna turned to him. He saw that her green eyes were almost blue.

So you are a ranger here, she said with a slight accent. Hanna had taken in the khaki shirt with the National Parks patch on his sleeve: arrowhead, Sequoia tree, bison and distant mountains. He also had the Stetson which kids liked to refer to as a Smokey the Bear hat, and was wearing the standard issue green trousers. Sam was proud of this uniform but now he felt stiff and official. Hanna was wearing a T-shirt with no bra and a short skirt with a slit up the back. He could see the lilac edge of her panties when she turned back to stare at the trees. In contrast, her socks were wool and her hiking boots, sturdy.

You are very lucky to have this job. On the other hand, I might be overwhelmed surrounded by this magnificence. Perhaps you are like a priest who after many years in the presence of God, realizes His grandeur relies on distance.

Sam wasn't certain exactly what she meant but it made him laugh and of course, he was intrigued. He arranged to meet her, after his shift, at the lodge where she was staying. They could have dinner together.

Their table was close to the stone fireplace but they also had an unobstructed view through the tall windows to the mountains.

I'm here for six months from Stockholm. I'm travelling on my own around America. I've done the east and the mid-west. I like this coast much better—Seattle, Portland, San Francisco, L.A. This is my last stop. Are you from California?

Yes, and I've done some travelling as well, though I've not been to Sweden. But I've never seen a place I wanted to be more than here.

The trees. I admire them too. In Stockholm I was involved in a protest. The government wanted to cut down thirteen elms to make way for a subway entrance. I was a tree-sitter. Spent a few nights in the branches so they couldn't use their chainsaws. Do you know? It was a successful action. The elms were saved.

That's wonderful. You were brave to take that on. Are you a student now, or will you be going to work?

I finished my undergraduate degree in textile arts. I was particularly interested in weaving but when I get back, I'm planning to do a masters in design.

After dinner, she invited him to her room. It was rustic and simple. He pulled her to him and put his hands through the slit in her skirt. The forest was framed in the open windows and the faint rustle of leaves could be heard in the still air. The room grew darker and Hanna lay down on the bed. For a moment he lost sight of her but she was calling: *Come to me.*

In the morning they arranged to meet for lunch. Sam brought bacon and tomato sandwiches. He took the afternoon off and drove her to the Mariposa Grove to see the Wawona Tunnel Tree. As a conservationist, Sam knew the negative impact of putting a hole in the base of a tree so that a car could pass through, but it had been done years ago. He wanted to show her the Washington tree, one of the largest in the world.

They ate lunch at a picnic table by the Wawona and then Sam drove south and parked near the trail to the Mariposa Grove. They had almost reached the Washington when Hanna said she had to take a bathroom break. *Don't worry, I always travel with some toilet paper in my pocket. I'll just go off the trail far enough for nobody to see me.*

Sam waited for ten minutes before he began to get anxious, then felt a terrible foreboding at fifteen. He started into the forest to find her but had only gone a few feet when she appeared.

I'm sorry. Hanna seemed distraught. *I saw the most colossal tree and walked over to it. It was almost like a magnet and I couldn't bring myself to leave. I kept touching the bark, telling the tree how special it was. It was the strangest sensation. The tree seemed to embrace me even though I know this is impossible. I felt I had to exert myself in the most physical way to detach from its grip. And then I began heading north. I knew I was going the wrong way from the position of the sun, so I turned around and came back making sure to take a route among the smaller trees.*

Sam held her for a few minutes until she was calmer and did not mention that he had the illusion of having been here with her previously. They continued their walk to the Washington tree and stood quietly admiring it before returning to the car.

★

Hanna was taking a red-eye back to New York with a connecting flight to Stockholm.

I feel so close to you which may be absurd after such a short time but you seem like my soul mate, Hanna admitted as they were taking leave of each other. Sam who usually dismissed "new age" rhetoric had to admit there *had* been something extraordinary in their connection. He felt deeply attached to her.

I miss you already but we'll phone and write often. You must come back soon. Perhaps at Christmas?

Definitely, I'll plan for that.

Sam called the next evening. The number Hanna had given him was not in service. He tried again two more times. The message was the same. Sam must have taken it down incorrectly. He wrote her a letter instead.

> *My Darling Hanna,*
> *You appeared to me like a sprite in the forest. I believe it is no exaggeration when I say I felt love for you almost immediately. I hope we can explore and deepen that love. I want to hear all the details of your life, how you spend your day, what you are reading, who you are talking with. I am interested in knowing who you are. I did try to call you, but the number was not connected. Perhaps you can send it to me again. Please write back quickly, or better still, phone me. I need to hear your voice.*
> *To our future,*
> *Sam.*

When after a few weeks no letter came from Hanna, he sent another. Sam wrote weekly for a while, never receiving a reply, then gave up.

Sam began to tire of his job which no longer had the magic factor that had always energized him. He began to search for other employment, applying to an ad for a Forestry Supervisor at the Grassy Narrows site logged by Weyerhaeuser. They were clearcutting aspen and birch for their mill. The position paid twice what he was earning.

The giant Sequoia, the one that was mutilated so that cars could drive through it, finally fell. Torrential rains hit California and the tree toppled.

THANKSGIVING

G ani and I are watching the Macy's Thanksgiving Day parade which goes right by my rent-controlled building. There is a huge balloon of a superhero and a colourful caterpillar from a children's storybook. I remember other years when there were turkey and clown balloons. I ask Gani to open the window, when the marching band comes by, so I can hear the trumpets. Gani buttons up her sweater. I have remained tolerant of the cold having grown up in a train station near White River in northern Ontario.

I know that in the 1920s, in the early years of the parade, they displayed live animals from the Central Park Zoo. It reminded me of the baby animals my father brought into the house after he killed their mothers. There was definitely a black bear in the basement for a few weeks but I especially remember the beavers who thought the Aladdin oil lamp was the moon.

Urbanites don't understand hunting. Daddy taught me to shoot because we relied on game for food. My first kill was a partridge. Shot it right in the eye. That's how good my aim was.

I wonder what will happen if Macy's closes. Who will sponsor the parade? Could happen. Bendel's is gone, Lord & Taylor, Bownwit Teller, B. Altman. The young people don't seem to care. My grandkids buy their torn jeans off the internet. When they come from California to visit, they won't set foot in a department store—*that's for old ladies*, they say, *no offense, Grandma*.

I like nice clothes. Blue is my favourite colour and cashmere is my favourite fabric. I hate slacks and only wear skirts, preferably pleated wool plaids. They've always suited me. Gani sent a package of my high heels to her relatives. I can only wear flats now. I have an amber necklace I keep handy, but most of my jewelry is in a safety deposit box. And my wedding ring is there, even though I've been divorced forever. Blake didn't want to move to the States.

As if to hide her slim body, Gani always wears loose pants and a sweatshirt. I think she had a bad experience when she worked in Saudi Arabia because she won't talk about her time there. She doesn't like to share much, but she did show me pictures of her wedding. I haven't seen a dress like that since the 1950s.

When the band is out of sight, Gani shuts the window. We watch a little longer and she starts to tell me about some celebration in the Philippines. I have to sit down because I'm gasping and need to get back to my oxygen tank before I pass out. She helps me get seated on the couch and places the cannula back in my nose. I adjust it slightly. *The doctors say my heart capacity is at twenty to thirty percent and they say I can't build it up. I need a miracle!*

Gani describes the festival in honour of Santo Nino. On her laptop I see the crowds dressed in red and gold costumes dancing and singing, hear the music and watch the wooden statue being paraded through the streets. It's a foot high, doll-like, brown faced, cherubic Christ child, elaborately garbed like a Spanish monarch. Gani tells me that her cousin worked for the church and watched the priests undress the statue at the end of the festival as prayers were recited. There is a drum roll each time an item is removed: crown, cape, tunic, boots, orb and sceptre. It is done to demonstrate the saviour's humility.

I want to practice the piano before lunch. Gani helps me wheel the oxygen tank to the bench. I play some drills then move on to Chopin's Prelude in C minor. It's a less demanding piece and all I can manage today. When lunch is ready, Gani helps me into the kitchen. She puts two plates filled with chicken and rice onto the table. My hands shake slightly but I can manage a knife and fork.

My mother cooked between arrivals, making blueberry pies and baking breads, careful not to miss a telegraph order so that my father knew if the train was going through or had to be directed onto a siding. Gani told me that when her family lived on a coconut farm they had plenty to eat but after the typhoon they had to move to the city and often went hungry. *We ate dog, Mrs. Cathcart*, she admitted. *I'm ashamed to tell anyone here. Americans love their pets so much.*

The station was my world when I was young. I completed elementary school by correspondence. Occasionally, a teacher stopped by in a train car to help with my homework. There were only three families besides ours. The maintenance men's kids were my playmates. I learned French that way.

For high school I had to go to the convent in town. I took the number two train on Sundays and came home Fridays on the number eight. I learned to play the piano there. I remember the music teacher was nice but some of the nuns were mean and made me eat raw eggs if they felt I needed discipline.

When I graduated, I moved down to Toronto and got my degree from the Faculty of Music at the university. Gani told me she only went to grade six. She's smart as a whip though and can speak three languages—Tagalog, Arabic and English.

After lunch, Gani assists in the bathroom. My balance is going so she makes sure I'm sitting in a stable position and helps me get on and off the toilet. It's time for my pills and she counts them out and brings me a glass of water. My swallow reflex is still okay so I down them easily.

I like to have a nap after eating. Gani wheels my oxygen tank to the sofa. My ankles are swollen so she lifts my legs when I want to lie down, and pulls the blanket up. I fall asleep quickly. I'm so tired these days.

It is getting dark out when I awake. I've slept the whole afternoon but that's not unusual. I ask Gani to put on a record. I've organized them so that several Bach albums, are on top. It's mostly what I listen to now. I'm glad I moved to New York with my children. I gave private piano lessons. Arlene seemed gifted and Darren was quite talented as well. I wanted them to learn from the best, like Richard Goode or Ann Schein. I myself took a few master classes but I was not at the concert level. Turned out my children weren't either. But I never regretted living in Manhattan although both of my children transferred to the west coast.

It's a little lonely just as it was when I was growing up. We were isolated with thick forests surrounding the small clearing. My mother wasn't affectionate. Once when I tried to kiss her, she bit my lip until it bled.

My dad sometimes took me out in the hand-pumped section car when he was doing track inspections. My mother warned him to be careful, but I was always somewhat disappointed that there were no close calls. What a thrill it was to imagine ditching at the last minute just before the train struck and crushed us.

I listen to *Sheep May Safely Graze,* one of fifteen movements in the *Hunting Cantata,* written for the Duke. An old photo album is on the side table and I flip through it as I have so often lately. Here is the kitchen with snow that drifted under the door. There is my sister, Thea, who died young. There I am in my old age in a purple velvet chair. I'm wearing shorts and a sleeveless blouse. On my hands are beaver fur mittens and I've got a fox stole around my neck, complete with head. These were tanned by my father. My daughter-in-law took the pictures and says I look like someone in a Diane Arbus shoot.

It's time for supper. I'm not very hungry so Gani makes me a tuna fish sandwich and puts it on a tray table in front of the TV. I watch the news but it is so dispiriting that I wish Gani would change the station. She's busy in her room, on the phone, talking in rapid-fire Tagalog to one of her friends. I watch a while longer. There are so many commercials I can barely stand it. My grandson says I should use the PVR or subscribe to Netflix but during his short stay, he never got around to showing me how.

Gani comes to get me ready for bed. It's a familiar routine— bathroom, pills, hearing aids out, oxygen tank. I lift my arms so Gani can remove my clothing. There is no drum roll, no fanfare but I feel humbled. She helps me on with my nightgown. It is then that I pinch her arm so hard she gasps in pain. She has to slap my hand away to calm me down.

WELLAND CANAL

One bottle of aspirin did the trick. Scruff was a small dog and Jim had no money for a vet to euthanize him. In fact, no vet would put him down. He wasn't old or sick. But Jim couldn't find anyone to take the dog. Scruff was a beauty. Handsome head, lean body and gorgeous coat, but he was skittish and couldn't stay still. He had been caged for months on a farm, and had only been let out occasionally to catch vermin in the barn.

When Jim rescued him and brought him home, Scruff couldn't get used to the freedom of the house. A few people had answered the ad Jim put on the Jack Russell website. But Scruff kept jumping on them and running a circuit from the couch to the chairs to the door, leaping onto the coffee table and back to the couch. He didn't answer to *down* or *sit* or anything else and people understood he was untrainable. A couple even came all the way from Toronto and Jim could see they liked the dog. But then the talk turned to how long it would take for Scruff to learn some obedience commands and how much money it would cost to get him the shots needed. He'd have to be neutered as well. Jim knew they wouldn't get in touch again and they didn't.

Jim had a deep love of dogs. When he was growing up in Welland, in the matchbox house he still lived in after his parents died, he didn't have much of anything but he always had a dog. After he got a job, he bought two Shepherds and treated them like kids. On the weekends they walked the length of the canal— miles from one end to the other. He had Clem for fifteen years and Track for twelve. Over the years, a couple of attractive women came and went. He thought Colleen was a keeper but she walked out one day after a fight. He couldn't remember now, what it was about. Then there was the one year gap while Jim was getting the treatments.

Scruff wasn't nippy. He didn't bark, but still nobody wanted him. Shame how that was. A good animal gone to waste and

young too, just over two years. When the doorbell rang, Scruff
was wrapped in a towel in the bathroom.

Morning, Jim. Where's Scruff?

It was his neighbour Marg who agreed to walk the dog at
eight each morning because Jim got short of breath in a hurry.
Scruff was usually right at the door ready to go. Jim decided to
tell Marg the truth because she'd been through the wringer like
him and wasn't one to judge.

Had to put him down.

What d'you mean?

*He's dead. Gave him a bottle of aspirin because nobody would have
him.*

Better that way, I guess, said Marg, who'd shifted between several foster families as a young girl.

I'm deciding what to do with the body.

Marg moved in view of the kitchen window that looked out
to the small patch of grass in the rear. There was an old fashioned
clothes line with some shirts hanging on it. She had to hand it to
him. Even though the place stank of tobacco smoke, Jim took
good care of his stuff and the bathroom was spotless. Reform
school had given him that discipline—hospital corners and all the
rest.

You could bury him in the yard, Marg said.

Yeah. I need to think on this.

Jim sat down in the lounge chair. Marg sat on the less saggy
part of the sofa. The living room was small by any standard. His
parents originally had a bigger place but it was expropriated when
they built the by-pass section of the canal. People joked that the
land wasn't even good for growing skunks but it had been their
home.

It was a petty theft charge that landed him in lock up. His
Dad, who had a steady job at Atlas Steel, said Jim was a good for
nothing, but the Salvation Army had gone to court with him and
persuaded the judge he wasn't a bad kid, so he only did six
months.

Remember Weaver's store on Main Street? he asked Marg. He
was in a reminiscing type of mood these days.

Yes, the one with the candy counter, Marg smiled.

Stole a couple of chocolate bars and old man Weaver called the cops on me.

Bastard.

Didn't even have a nickel to buy them.

I stole candy from him every week. Never got caught.

She looked over at Jim. He was skeleton thin and his face had no colour.

His words came out as if he was speaking through sandpaper.

How've you been feeling? Marg asked.

The beard's coming in and the hair's growing back. He ran his fingers through the long, grey strands that touched his shoulders.

All the docs say it's the cigarettes not the asbestos. But I don't know. Thirty years in the mill and all that exposure.

Can't trust them, for sure. Marg didn't like to think about the sterilization after that first baby. And damn it, now the tears were welling up. Her sweet, sweet girl snatched away, and no chance for another.

I didn't want Scruff to end up at the pound. Not to get morbid or anything, but they'd kill him there anyway.

You did what you had to do. I'd have taken him if it weren't for the cats. With six of them running around it would have been just too much. Come over for supper tomorrow. I'll cook up some chili.

Marg had worked at the cotton mill until she was laid off in the 1980s. She'd been on the pogey ever since and knew how to stretch her food budget.

Sounds good.

Jim went to check on Scruff. It wasn't wrong to use the word peaceful for the dead. Scruff looked fully at rest and was that such a bad thing?

*

Jim grabbed his jacket and car keys and drove the pickup truck over to Calvin's stone yard.

Hey, Cal, how's it going, Jim rasped.

Can't complain, man.

I need a couple of rocks—trying to keep the damn neighbours from messing up my grass when they come home drunk and drive over my lawn.

What size you looking for?

Something pretty big but I gotta be able to carry them.

Cal looked at Jim's fragile frame.

Come on over here. What d'ya think?

Looks doable.

Jim lifted one of the rocks. It was heavier than he expected.

I'll just back the truck a touch closer.

He chose three rocks and lifted them onto the flat bed himself. He thought he might pass out at one point, but he managed to get the job done.

Thanks, Cal. See you, buddy.

Jim left the rocks in the truck.

He ate a decent supper, fried up some ground meat and potatoes to keep his strength up.

He collected Scruff from the floor of the bathroom and set him on the seat beside him in the truck. He drove to a remote section of the canal where a break in the barrier was surrounded by orange cones, and marked with yellow tape.

Jim remembered the thrill of his teenage years when he jumped off the twelve foot wall into the canal. A couple of girls from the high school would be standing around watching, glancing at the bulge in his bathing suit as he strutted along the top of the wall waiting for the perfect moment to leap. He was glad he had taken that risk. He thought of the cold shock of hitting the water. When he surfaced the girls were still there. He remembered the name of one of the girls, Donna. He'd taken her to Merritt Park after dark where they lay under a picnic table and necked.

Jim took Scruff in his arms, set him down and rolled the rocks out of the truck onto the ground. He uncoiled a sturdy length of rope and tied the dog to one rock. With a series of knots, he secured two other pieces of rope to the two remaining rocks and to each of his ankles. With great effort and with Scruff in his arms he slowly shuffled and dragged himself to the edge of the canal. After the terror, he believed there could be that moment of exhilaration.

ACKNOWLEDGMENTS

Thank you to Chris Needham for reminding me that now means now. Much appreciation for Ann Atkey's editing expertise. A nod to the Leaside Library writing group. With gratitude to Bruce for unwavering support.